John Burd

How People Manage Things in Manchester

Sir. E.A. as a trustee

John Burd

How People Manage Things in Manchester
Sir. E.A. as a trustee

ISBN/EAN: 9783337363635

Printed in Europe, USA, Canada, Australia, Japan

Cover: Foto ©Andreas Hilbeck / pixelio.de

More available books at **www.hansebooks.com**

HOW PEOPLE MANAGE THINGS

IN MANCHESTER;

OR,

SIR E. A. AS A TRUSTEE.

BY

JOHN BURD,

MOUNT SION, RADCLIFFE, LANCASHIRE.

LONDON:

PRINTED FOR THE AUTHOR.

1866.

TO THE PUBLIC.

In making known at some length the circumstances relating to a great individual oppression, the author feels disposed to turn the occasion to some account for the good of others. The great and increasing difficulties attending the prosecution of trade, render it necessary and desirable that those difficulties should not be increased by the state of the law. The condition of the people-question requires that every restraint upon the industry of the people should be removed. The absurd state of our monetary laws is the most crying abuse from which the country suffers. No temporary measures will do ; it will be proper to search out to the foundation the whole system of currency and credit. The principle must be laid down, that the interests and welfare of the great masses of the people must be consulted and provided for. This must not be by sacrificing one class for the sake of another, but by an equal law for every class. The present law is most arbitrary, oppressive, unequal, and unjust. The whole system of trade is made needlessly dangerous and anxious by it. The whole labour market is depreciated by the operation of the present law. Great multitudes are kept in idleness, and therefore in misery, and exposed to crime, by the fierce pressure of our monetary laws. Men, however good, however industrious, and however worthy of confidence, are commercially dead, if not possessed of a balance at the bank. Their position is one of absolute slavery, and they cannot be redeemed from that condition, except at the will and according to the caprice of the moneyed class. All pretences to liberty and independence are ignored by the present system. Many servants are slaves ; their comfort, nay, their existence, beyond a workhouse or a prison, depends upon the smile, and may be destroyed by the frown, of their fellow man. A man without property cannot trade, and therefore cannot live, except by selling his labour to others. How cruel a law, to put into the hands of one class the absolute disposal of all the rest of the inhabitants! The moneyed class can crush down the labour market to any extent which their tyranny or heartlessness may allow,—they hold in their hands the means of supplying the rest of the community with work, and therefore with bread;—at their arbitrary pleasure they can close their pockets, and let the masses starve; and there is no one to bid them nay. How is this? It is because, in the eye of the law, property is everything, and men are nothing. This is the fundamental error, and it is for the representatives of the people to remove the stumbling-block; and the man who passes a measure effectually to remove the abuses of the present system, will deserve well of his country, and have earned a title to the highest rewards it can confer. Let her Majesty's reign receive its most illustrious distinction by a reform of our money laws. As the late Prince Consort rejoiced on the passing of the Corn Law Abolition Bill, because it gave cheap bread to the people, so may her Majesty have reason to rejoice over the blessed results due to the passing of a bill, giving freedom to the trade in money, as well as in corn. Such a measure will raise our masses from their deep degradation; give hope to the industrious, because they will not only have work, but a due reward for their toil; make the paying of the taxes an easy matter; and diffuse universal content and physical well-being over the nation. Let all patriots, and all who have a stake in the country, unite their efforts for the passing through Parliament of a wise and complete measure, to relieve the trade and industry of the land from the pressure of the present law. In seeking relief for an individual grievance, the author would rejoice if in any degree he should be successful in pointing out a national evil, and crying out for its remedy. The nation is made up of individuals. Let individual wrongs be redressed, and let justice be done by every part of the nation to every other part, and the whole nation will then be able to rejoice together.

"HOW PEOPLE MANAGE THINGS IN MANCHESTER;"

OR, SIR E. A. AS A TRUSTEE.

Sir E. A., of H. H., E., and Mr. W. B., of A., were left by the late Mr. Alderman B., of H., as Trustees to his estate. Mr. Alderman B. died on the 18th August, 1848. On the 30th September, 1848, his eldest son, Mr. W. B., of M. B., died, aged 30 years. All these parties resided in the neighborhood of Manchester. Mr. W. S., of Messrs. S., W., and Co., Solicitors, Manchester, and a connection, by marriage, of Mr. Cobden's, the apostle of free trade, made the will. Immediately after Mr. B.'s interment, and before the death of Mr. W. B., all the members of the family were assembled, together with the Trustees. Sir E. A. requested that Mr. J. N., solicitor, might be elected to act as legal adviser to the Trustees in all matters which concerned them in the place of Mr. W. S. This proposal was assented to by all parties concerned. At the time of his death, Mr. Alderman B. was in partnership with his two eldest sons. The business of printing was carried on at Mount S., R., and the vending of the goods printed at the warehouse in Manchester. By the provisions of the will, the two surviving partners had the option of purchasing the business on certain terms, and six weeks were allowed after the death of Mr. B., as the time for their consideration whether they would purchase it. About a month after the death of Mr. Alderman B., his eldest son, Mr. W. B., fell ill and died, as before stated; in consequence of this circumstance, all attention was diverted from the consideration of the purchase of the business, and was fixed upon the dangerous illness of Mr. W. B.

After his death and burial, the question of the purchase of the business was revived. Mr. S. B., banker, of Manchester, was left as the Trustee to the estate of Mr. W. B.; Mr. J. B. of Mount S., R., was the surviving partner, and the second son of Mr. Alderman B. He had on his hands to deal with two estates and their Trustees. If the Trustees did not pull together, how dangerous was his position. He entered into an understanding with Mr. S. B. to pay out of the concern, at certain dates, the money belonging to the separate estate of Mr. W. B.; he elected to purchase the business of his father upon the terms specified in the will. The death of Mr. W. B. having in the mean-time elapsed, and the period having passed over during which the option was permitted to be exercised for the purchase of the business, the Trustees refused to agree to allow Mr. J. B. to have the business. Sir E. A. shrunk from the responsibility of breaking up the business; Mr. S. B. urged upon Sir. E. A. to do so;—he wished to avoid the odium attached to such a course of proceeding. The Court of Chancery was appealed to, and permission obtained to sell the business to Mr. J. B. After the sanction of the Court of Chancery was obtained, Sir E. A. requested that Mr. W. B. might be allowed, at a salary, to conduct the business at the Manchester end, and thus, virtually, have the Trustees embarked in the business. Mr. S. B. decidedly condemned this proposal; and after it was agreed upon, refused to be the banker of the concern, as it was a course of action contrary to his opinion; Sir E. A. insisted so positively upon this appointment, that although Mr. J. B. was exceedingly unwilling to do anything contrary to Mr. S. B.'s opinion, Sir E. A. was allowed to have his own way. Sir E. A. introduced Mr. J. B. to the Manchester and Salford Bank, and the Manchester and Salford Bank, in conjunction with the Bank of England, were the bankers for the concern. All went well as long as Mr. J. N. lived; the business prospered, a great deal of money was made, the business was extended, and there was every reason for congratulation and thankfulness.

Commerce was in a highly prosperous state at the time when the Russian war broke out; a profitable trade was carried on abroad with many foreign markets, and merchants generally were satisfied with the results of their operations. The commencement of hostilities changed this happy condition of things, and gradually brought many miseries in its train. The demand for goods was interrupted, and soon, in many instances, indefinitely broken off. The producers of goods soon felt the change ; their accustomed outlets for goods were stopped, and a severe competition for the remaining markets followed. The usual profits of trade were not realized, and much apprehension ensued. Unfortunately, this panic feeling was communicated to the Trustees in an inordinate degree, and induced, on their part, a recklessness which led to most painful consequences. It brought on a fight between Mr. Alderman B.'s Trustees on the one hand, and Mr. W. B.'s Trustee on the other. The original provocation came from Sir E. A. ; without consulting Mr. S. B., or obtaining his consent, Sir E. A. resolved to prevent the arrangement with Mr. S. B. as to the paying out of the concern of Mr. W. B.'s money from being carried into effect. He had been a consenting party to the arrangement, and was bound by it ; if he had wished the arrangement to have been altered, he ought to have sought to have done so by negociation ;—he took the violent method, and did the greatest injury to the business. Mr. W. B. was engaged under a signed agreement to Mr. J. B. to serve him faithfully; Sir E. A. induced Mr. W. B. to break his agreement with Mr. J. B., and to violate the arrangement entered into with Mr. S. B.; and so to arouse his wrath, that afterwards, Mr. S. B. never was the same man as long as he lived. Mr. S. B. entered into an action against the concern, and compelled Mr. Alderman B.'s Trustees to allow payment to be made. The consequences did not end there,—it broke up the harmony which had always existed before, and produced a strife, the effects of which are now felt in full force.

This collision of the Trustees was noised abroad, and a great injury was done to the trading position of the concern. The damage that had accrued was from a reputed friend, and not from an enemy. All the Trustees had become heated by passion, and each endeavored to excel the other in the perversity and unreasonableness of their conduct. No injury ever came to the business except from the attacks of false friends; and blows struck from the interior of a business are always the most deadly.

After Mr. J. N.'s death, Sir E. A., entirely upon his own authority, and without consulting anybody, went to Messrs. S., H., & Co.'s, and constituted Mr. S. H. as the legal adviser to the Trustees. Thus a total stranger was brought into contact with the business, without the consent and against the will of the parties interested in the property. Mr. S. H., instead of seeking to have his position legalised, and to promote the concord and welfare of the whole family, began to sow division wherever he could, and became the private partizan of Sir E. A. The system of exciting differences amongst the Trustees inaugurated his position as legal adviser to the Trustees. He induced Sir E. A. to enter upon this hostile course; Sir E. A. induced Mr. W. B. to betray his employer, and strike a mortal blow at his dearest interests. Thus strife was introduced, and eventually total ruin was brought down upon a noble business.

The credit of the business was greatly injured by this *émeute* amongst the Trustees, and the confidence which had universally been established was greatly weakened in tone. The Manchester and Salford Bank were astonished at the conduct and behaviour of Sir E. A., and became suspicious and distrustful in their behaviour. For a period trade got worse and worse. The business was in crack trading order, perfectly organized, and every way adapted to do well. The concern was greatly enlarged, many valuable business connections were established, and it only required the manifestation on the part of the Trustees of patience and perseverance, for a few years, to place the business in the very first rank in the town.

After the death of Mr. J. N., who had been their guide and friend, the Trustees seemed to lose the excellent spirit by which they had been actuated, and which had produced such capital effects; and under other counsels, another *régime* was established. The change was very adverse. Competition became intense; other concerns were absorbing the business at prices much below cost, and lessening employment from day to day. Instead of acting with due circumspection and caution, Sir E. A. lost his head, and became bowed down with fear; —terror got full possession of his mind, and drove reason from its seat. This state of things was much to be regretted. The painstaking labor of forty years was not considered;—the welfare of his departed friend's wife and children was disregarded. The battle had been fought; the victory had been won; and the supposed difficulties had been surmounted. With continuance in the same policy, the brows of Sir E. A. might have been crowned with laurel, as the honest man, as the upright administrator, and the sincere and faithful friend. Unhappily for himself, and unhappily for those whose interests he represented, he chose a different path, and forsook the path of uprightness. He "did run well, what did hinder him?" In matters of lesser as of greater importance, "he that endureth to the end shall be saved." How much to be deplored, that he should hold in his hands the interests of those whom he injured so deeply and so desperately, and all for want of a little courage and manfulness in the faithful and conscientious discharge of a very solemn duty.

The conduct of Sir E. A. shewed that his feelings had undergone a complete revolution; in fact, he was at this time, a dangerous and unscrupulous enemy. Instead of endeavouring to respect the rights and properties of other parties, he became completely indifferent and absolutely reckless. Instead of endeavouring to avoid and escape danger, he seemed resolved to seek it, and determined to have it; his mind was poisoned. He did not stop to consider the effects of his behaviour; so uncontrollable was the power of prejudice over him, that he did not ask himself where he was going to, and in what position he would place the interests committed to his hand. The property of others had been placed in his care on the faith of his respecting the covenants into which he had entered; Sir E. A.'s conduct was most unworthy. The public had placed property in the hand of the concern, and were willing to place ten times as much, on the faith of Sir E. A. regarding the duties which he had undertaken to discharge. Why, without reason or necessity, he should arbitrarily enter upon a course so unworthy, and forsake the paths of rectitude and honour, has always been a mystery, and is so now to this day. By what means were filched away from his mind all regard to truth and fair-play, all respect for himself, all love for his departed friend, all consideration for his own professions and promises; and why he should, at all risks, force another man, and the interests of other persons, into a course of repudiation simply because he had the power and opportunity to do so, he must himself explain and excuse, by what means he thinks proper to use. Without previous enquiry, and without notice, suddenly he pulled up the concern, stopped its traffic, and put an extinguisher on its prosperity and progress; thus Sir E. A. slipped from friendship into malice, from the path of duty into a method of obstruction and mischief. He acted thus by the influence of Mr. S. H.

The feeling which had produced this catastrophe, carried matters along in the same course. Sir E. A. had outraged every feeling of common sense;—he had sacrificed the principle of honour. That principle which backs a man in the fulfilment of duty, Sir E. A. had sneered at and despised, and so sacrificed the respect of the commercial community. Even at this juncture, if he would have retraced his steps and pursued the path of integrity, he had the proffer of universal sympathy and assistance. He chose otherwise, and the trading public soon opened his eyes to the fact that repudiation does not pay. He had offended old and long-tried friends, and sacrificed all the friendships which had grown up with the business; and made the concern excessively unpopular, and transactions exceedingly difficult to effect. A meeting was held of all the parties who were interested in the concern. Sir E. A. had turned the concern completely over, and forfeited its good name. He had taken an effectual step in its destruction, and now he proceeded to take a second step. Mr. J. B., regretting the course the Trustees had taken, submitted a proposal, to the effect that time should be given, so that the concern might pay all claims with interest; and offering to allow, in the meantime, an inspection of its operations. The Trustees, by their solicitor, overruled all proposals, through a threat of bankruptcy proceedings held over the meeting, and compelled the trade creditors eventually to forego part of their claims. Mr. S. H. deceived all parties who had been in the habit of trading with the concern, and what is exceedingly curious, also wrested from them their assent. He deprived them of nine shillings in the pound, and spread over the payment of the eleven shillings in the pound, without paying interest, during two years. Many, and loud, and bitter were the complaints on account of this course of proceeding. This act of confiscation was consummated at a second meeting, when Sir E. A. was present—as he did not venture to shew himself at the first meeting, on account of the disgraceful part he had to play, but ran away to London, leaving Mr. S. H. to fight the battle without him, alone.

The Trustees had been exceedingly busy, running about, canvassing here and there, in order to carry out their proposal. Their position was a false one, on account of the part they acted. They made an application to Chancery, in order to have all their proceedings endorsed, and so endeavour to free themselves from liability. Their course at this juncture was interrupted by Mr. C. S. S., who had married the youngest daughter of Mr. Alderman B.; he determined to turn things to his own advantage, and did this in such a manner as to prove himself to be a fit coadjutor with Sir E. A. himself. Resolving to secure himself, and not caring for anyone, he insisted upon being paid preferentially his wife's total claim. He threatened to make the Trustees responsible, but he did it in such an offensive way to everybody, that no one would coalesce with him for the consummation of his threat. How did the

Trustees act in this straight? They taxed the jointure of the widow of the late Mr. Alderman B. with a life insurance policy to secure to Mr. C. S. S. a collateral security, and by this means bought off Mr. C. S. S.'s opposition at the widow's expense. Thus the rich executor acted towards the poor widow, and deprived her for the remainder of her life of three-fourths of the annuity her husband had left for her support. Mr. C. S. S. having thus extorted from the fears of Sir E. A. this arrangement, then entered secretly into a kind of alliance with the Trustees, to annoy, and vex, and obstruct the progress of the concern. A conclave was held, and opportunity was seized hold of, in applying to Chancery to obtain an agreement ostensibly for the future regulation of the business. The checks which Sir E. A. had experienced, and the criticism to which he exposed himself, irritated his temper to such an extent, that his passions completely mastered him. His power was now unrestrained; and his malice, spite, prejudice, and hatred, broke out with overwhelming violence. He took occasion to devise an instrument in conjunction with Mr. S. H., Mr. W. S., and Mr. C. S. S., of a character as for ever to stamp him one of the meanest and most tyrannical of mankind. It has only to be read in order to provoke the indignation of all business men, and to cover its authors with disgrace. Its provisions betray so much ignorance of commerce, and the way in which it ought to be transacted, that it is a question whether its perusal excites more the surprise or the sense of the ridiculous in the mind of the reader. It seems to embody all the evil with which the feelings of Sir E. A. had become embittered. Sir E. A. seemed to call to his aid every means to pour on the head of Mr. J. B. all the vials of his wrath. He wished to place upon Mr. J. B. a galling yoke, with the view of crushing him down in anguish and despair. Sir E. A. plunged into error after error, in one endless scene of folly, confusion, and resentment. Obstinately pursuing his own way, he altered what was right to wrong; was angry with the effects of the wrong thing he had done, and then went farther wrong. He wanted indelibly to fix on Mr. J. B. all the responsibility and blame of the policy which he had so wilfully practised; and he seemed unwearied in pursuing the principal victim of his cruelty, with all the persecution which a depraved heart could conceive, and carry into effect. In this policy Sir E. A. never wavered nor faltered, until he had plunged everything into a total ruin.

It was generally supposed that the business would be left intact;

that its usual course would be followed; and nothing done to injure or obstruct its progress. The reality turned out to be absolutely different. The rights of the proprietor were sought to be invaded, and an endeavor was made entirely to throw them aside. The new arrangements produced great changes in the condition and prospects of the business.

At the time Sir E. A. stopped the concern, the lease of the printworks had rather more than two years to run. Mr. S. H. had set his heart upon making a new lease, and breaking the old one. Mr. S. H. was solicitor to the Earl of W.; and the only thing he cared for, was to protect the interest of his principal client. For this end, he would sacrifice every one else. It was a complicated arrangement to effect; inasmuch as Mr. W.'s lease ended at the same time Mr. J. B.'s lease did. Mr. W. had held from the Earl of W., and Mr. J. B. held from Mr. W. Mr. J. B. wished the lease he had to run to the end, in the usual way. Mr. S. H. objected to this course. He induced Sir E. A. to unite with him to compel Mr. W. and Mr. J. B. to break the old lease, and to take a fresh one dating back about two years before the old lease had run out. Mr. S. H. never cared for any other object than this; and when he had accomplished it, he showed his recklessness about everything else. Soon after this, he entered upon a mad course, and spited every one he was connected with, and should have been concerned for. He injured the landlord's interest, and the family interest; he almost annihilated the creditors' interest, and quite ruined the property and prospects of the owner. It is quite wonderful to consider how he could have contrived to do so much mischief. If he had displayed half the talent and energy to conduct the affairs of the concern to a prosperous result, he would have had to receive the thanks of every one. Instead of that, he erected himself into a very demon of perversity, and delighted in setting every one by the ears. Every obstruction he could contrive, was put in the way of the transaction of business; every difficulty he could raise, was magnified; and every objection he could suggest, was presented and pressed; in order that he might rule, and trample on the rights of every one anxious about the matter.

As soon as the fresh *régime* was established, the effect upon the credit of the concern was most marked. All the customers were disconcerted and timorous. Great losses followed this change of the administration, and much property was sacrificed. Mr. J. B.'s power and control of the business were destroyed, and he had no influence of a direct character. It was curious to see the demoralising effect upon the various servants employed. One after another seemed to become corrupted and spoiled. From the long working of the concern, there was not in the trade a better or more harmonious body of work-people. Their character and conduct rapidly deteriorated; and the excellent discipline which had so long prevailed, seemed to be relaxed and destroyed. Less work was done, and done in a worse manner. The cheerful emulation in the discharge of their duty had passed away, and a dogged carelessness and indifference were exhibited in the fulfilment of their obligations. Thus the perverseness in the policy and practice of the Trustees, was strongly marked in its operation upon the *employés* engaged in the business; and produced annoyance, mischief, and injury, from time to time.

If the Trustees had been animated by integrity, they would have taken care to have arranged the conducting of the business so that no restriction should be placed on its progress, and no barrier in the way of its prosperity. Instead of this, the Trustees violated all the prece-dents of the concern. They had all the plans of a business which had been highly successful. Instead of treading vigorously in the old foot-steps, they would not act in conjunction with its old friends; and jeopardised the whole property by carrying the business into fresh channels, which were not prepared for, nor capable of sustaining it.

To manifest such a spirit of recklessness and childishness in the treatment of the property of other people, and to be so careless of everything, provided they came off scot-free, rendered the proceedings of the Trustees of the most foolish and dangerous character.

Instead of taking care to obtain from the Court of Chancery powers of a business-like character, the Trustees had acted with the greatest rashness and caprice. Although surrounded by those who could afford the soundest information, they preferred acting after their own judgments. They ought to have revived the concern, after all the adverse influences to which it had been exposed. They should have arranged financial matters so as not to cripple its operations. Every-thing should have been done to stimulate activity and reward progress. They had absorbed the powers of the business in their own hands; and what did they do with them? Everything was done to repress the action of the concern, and render the business difficult. It was the policy to starve and enfeeble its operations. It was desired only just to let it live, but to forbid a vigorous life. This behaviour on the part of men who held all the resources of the concern in their own power, was the most painful that can be conceived. If the Trustees were referred to on any business, their replies were evasive and uncertain. There was nothing hearty or sincere about them. Having knocked the concern down, they showed permanent bad feeling; but no candour, no regret for having done wrong, and no endeavour to do right for the future.

The Trustees were very fond of personal attention; but never gave any fair or reasonable behaviour in exchange. They were very fond of getting to know the opinions of every one else; but would not cooperate in a friendly spirit for the prosecution of business objects. Persons were continually finding out that no right use was made of trade communications; but employed in a totally unscrupulous manner to defeat right objects, and to advance a contrary policy, however opposed to the interest and welfare of the business. Their principles of action were so contrary to reason, as to make persons feel that they had in the Trustees unpitying and dangerous enemies. It was found to be dangerous to go to them with the complaint that anything was wrong, and with the view of having it ameliorated. Instead of attaining their object, persons were met with opposition and abuse. This kind of conduct coming from persons less informed than those technically instructed, and having a long and particular experience, was anything but agreeable. How could it be otherwise than that conduct, so ungentlemanly and unfair, should have the worst effects? Thus the Trustees got a cord tied round the throat of the concern, and most iniquitously did they use the power which they had so unrighteously obtained.

In this second application to Chancery, the Trustees had procured an instrument for the regulation of the business. In accordance with its provisions, Mr. J. B. had a formal part to take. Mr. J. B. had the nomination of the manager; while Sir. E. A. held a veto, and therefore could affirm it, or negative it, at his pleasure. Mr. W. B. having the track of the business in his hand, and being used to the customers, was the person most qualified to promote the interests of the business, and therefore best fitted to have the appointment. It appears that the Trustees had had a private quarrel amongst themselves, and Sir E. A. negatived the nomination. Mr. J. B. then nominated Mr. G. B. to fill the office of manager. Mr. G. B. was the youngest son of

Mr. Alderman B. ; was interested under the will, and therefore, from birth and position, very well fitted to fill the appointment with safety to all interests involved. His appointment would have been popular with the young men engaged in the business, and would have been sympathised with by the public. Sir E. A., however, absolutely refused to ratify this appointment. Sir E. A. seemed determined to exercise the power he possessed in the most offensive manner. He would give fair speeches, but his deeds were out of harmony with his words, and were of the most despotic type. Mr. J. B. then nominated the Works Manager. Sir E. A. again met the nomination with a point-blank refusal. Indeed, he seemed determined to refuse any one calculated to act well for the concern. What was to be done? A great establishment was standing in order to receive its governor, before trade could be proceeded with. In this juncture, Mr. W. S. brought forward a party who was accepted by Sir E. A. Mr. W. S. recommended him as a quiet, harmless man, who would not interfere with the business. He turned out to be too ignorant to be harmless ; and was also perverse and obstinate in his behaviour, and offensive in his manners. In course of time, he became a tool in the hands of the Trustees to do anything the Trustees wanted him to do, whether according to the decree of the Court of Chancery or not. His name was Mr. U. He had been a calico printer, and had quarrelled with his partner. He had embarked his capital in a business of which he was more ignorant than of his own; became an adventurer upon the tender mercies of the public to unfortunate men, and found Mr. W. S. merciful to him at Mr. J. B.'s expense.

The preparations were now complete. The Trustees had now gone through a long series of changes. They had had a most hazardous journey, and now they had a breathing time. Had they mended matters? They had upset the established order of things which had existed during many years, and had produced *admirable* results! These changes were not beneficial. The judgment of the Trustees was altogether at fault, and they had grievously erred. For the end they had gained, they had wasted a great deal of property, offended a great number of persons, and had pursued an utterly unscrupulous course. Did they now begin to reflect upon what they had done, and begin to act wisely? Unhappily the report of their proceedings manifests no improvement in their temper or their principles. Unhappy influences still prevailed in their counsels, and the results were as bad as could be prognosticated.

A very curious state of things now existed. Practically speaking, Sir E. A. was the head of the business, and Mr. U. was his principal agent. Mr. J. B.'s place in his own business was absolutely nominal; and, at a pinch, he could be positively entirely dispensed with. Did Sir E. A. really look after the interests of the business, the same as if it had been his own? He was accustomed to a business of an entirely different character, and he might at times be strangely perplexed with a trade so very different from his own. His business was a spinning and manufacturing business. He now entered upon the supervision of a bleaching, printing, and dyeing business. He had received no training, and possessed no information on the nature of the trade. In addition to this disadvantage, he left a large and important business entirely to servants; and very much they abused his confidence. There had been a quarrel between the Trustees. As a consequence, Sir E. A. would not give the principal position to Mr. W. B. Mr. W. B.'s pride was hurt, and he neglected his duty. He said he could not take the second place, and confessed he had neglected his duty. The Official Manager could not steer the ship. He could not be made to comprehend what the duties were he had to fulfil, and therefore never performed them. Mr. W. B.'s dereliction of duty, and the utter incapacity of the Manager, produced a loss of business, and consequently a loss of money. The Manager did not in any way respect the agreement for conducting the business; and continuing the same course without improvement, or adaptation of himself to the circumstances in which he was placed, both he and Mr. W. B. had to be dismissed. In proceeding to elect the successor, there was very little choice. The second Manager of the concern was a connection of Sir E. A.'s, and his name was Mr. H. This man had been a partner in a printing firm, which had broken down under disastrous circumstances. He had also been for many years responsible Manager of a print business; and that also broke down in his hands. Upon this man, Sir E. A. had set his heart. He proved to be entirely incapable of managing the business. What to do, he seemed entirely at a loss to know; and how to do it, was quite beyond his power. He finished the disarrangement which the previous Manager had commenced. He pulled down the old organization, and never substituted a fresh one. He wasted time, kept a large concern without work, was completely nonplussed, and could not extricate himself from embarrassment and difficulty. He was not at all fitted for this kind of business, for he did not understand it. He was a most careless, ignorant, procrastinating person; and Sir E. A. must have been exceedingly ashamed of having given him the appointment. He loved to carouse and amuse himself. Work he abhorred, and always desired to run away from. His stay involved a tremendous loss. He received a three months' notice to leave, and then ceased to interfere. The change was immediate. The concern seemed to be relieved from an incubus which pressed it down. The people engaged on the business did their duty; and the business sprung into life, and a good trade was done. There was daylight now, after a long period of darkness. The goodness of the concern, notwithstanding the mutilating process it had undergone, was now proved. It was now only necessary to pursue the right track, and the concern from this time would have made rapid strides and been crowned with triumphant success.

If Sir E. A. had now remedied the proved defects of the management agreement, or else dispensed with it entirely, he would have retrieved all his previous errors, and secured the property to its rightful owners. This reasonable line of conduct he would not follow; but persisted in carrying out the letter of the agreement, while he absolutely violated the spirit of it. If Sir E. A. had had one spark of feeling, or possessed one iota of right principle, he would not obstinately have carried on an arrangement shewn to be destructive to the energies of the business, and fatal to its existence. Both managers had entirely misunderstood the course they ought to have taken; and now it had been placed unmistakeably before Sir E. A. the way they ought to have followed. Both managers violated their obligations. They endeavoured to close the London and country trade; and thus shut off the concern from its most lucrative occupation, and most wealthy connexion. They endeavoured to throw the concern entirely into the hire business, and amongst a poor class of customers. This they did, by placing obstacles in the way of the execution of business which presented itself. Their conduct lost all appearance of propriety, and assumed a most violent form and character. Sir E. A. cast away the golden opportunity. He seemed exasperated in having to part with his protégé. It was of no use to shew his incapacity. He was deaf to all argument. When Mr. H.'s notice expired, no man could be found on the spur of the moment to fill the place; and Sir E. A. would not allow proper time to find a suitable person. He had the power, and he would have back again, notwithstanding his proved incapacity, the man he had first sanctioned. He had made up his mind now to be mischievous; and he was so. When Mr. U. came back again, was it found he had profited by his first dismission? Not in the least. The man had lost all susceptibility of improvement. Experience was lost on him. It did him no good whatever. Thus it is plain to be seen Sir E. A. again did wrong. He had been shewn the right way. He would not pursue it. By experience he had seen the errors he had made. It had been pointed out to him how he might escape those errors; and yet he followed them in preference to a right, and wise, and upright road. He would go the straight road to ruin and destruction.

The fact that Sir E. A. had got the concern in his own power, and that he could either make it or destroy it, was patent to all observers. He must therefore bear the responsibility which he allowed to come upon him, and answer at the bar of public opinion for all his misdeeds. He had by experiment seen proved before his eyes, that the concern was a first-rate one. He did not doubt it. Every pretence to misconception was done away with. It was clearly understood that the composition he had forced upon the creditors was wrong, and his interference with the concern itself a violation of personal rights. Yet notwithstanding this,—while he was convinced himself, and every one as well as himself likewise convinced, that, if he would fulfil the part he had undertaken to discharge, all would go well, and turn out successfully,—the resolution he took was quite the contrary. He seemed determined to ruin the business. He strove to do this secretly, and prevent all remark being made. He worked in the dark, and brought to bear his wicked intentions.

When Mr. U. returned, for a period of nine months the concern just kept its position, and neither made nor lost ground. The Trustees and the Manager were obliged to shew in their conduct an appearance of discretion. It had been demonstrated before many witnesses what the business could do, if it were properly handled. After this stationary condition, the concern again began to do well. The Manager, instead of quietly pursuing the road on which he was travelling, and with every promise of advantage, went entirely wrong. His conduct was, however, very difficult to explain. It was, indeed, quite inexplicable. How to account for it was a mystery. He had formed some plan in his own mind; but of what nature, did not immediately appear. Whether it came from himself, or was by the suggestion of another, never came to light. Instead of fulfilling his duty, quietly and perseveringly, he turned from the right path into crooked ways. He was evidently bent on breaking through all rules. There was a fixed purpose manifested entirely to depart from the management agreement. There seemed to be, on the part of the Trustees, a determination to back him in his conduct. There seemed to be an indifference as to what the manager did, and a disregard of all the regulations which the Trustees had forced into practice. The animus was exceedingly bad. There was great irritation, and all the manifestations of a storm. A conspiracy was hatching. The Manager wrote a letter to the Trustees, alleging complaints against Mr. J. B. Mr. J. B. replied to this communication, and shewed cause to the Trustees why he should be dismissed. He had broken, and continued to break, the provisions of the management agreement; and it was impossible to allow him to continue to do this.

At this time, raw materials rose rapidly in value, and disturbed the usual calm and regularity of business. Trade diminished for a time, and caused the margin between cost and profit to be obliterated. Also two persons failed, owing between them a considerable sum of money to the concern, and through whom the Manager had imprudently arranged to do a great deal of business, although warned both by Mr. S. B. and Mr. J. B. not to trust these parties. A great loss of money and a great loss of trade followed. Sir E. A. resolved to use this circumstance to put an end to the concern, and to make it of fatal effect. He had himself been the cause of this loss being incurred, in obstinately sticking to a management which had been repeatedly proved guilty of infractions of the agreement, which gave the powers to act. Sir E. A. still pursued an unworthy line of conduct. He daily committed unblushing violations of his engagements. He began to play fast and loose, and deferred from day to day the appointment of a new Manager, although continually solicited to do so. He kept referring Mr. J. B. to Mr. S. H. ; and Mr. S. H. kept referring Mr. J. B. to Sir E. A., bandying Mr. J. B. about between Mr. S. H. and himself, and, on the most frivolous grounds, keeping the question from a settlement. In the meantime the conduct of Mr. U. became so scandalous, and the injury to the business so outrageous, that it could only be explained by his having received secret instructions from Sir E. A. to this effect.

Mrs. B., the widow of Mr. Alderman B., paid a visit to Sir. E. A. to remonstrate with him on the violation of his agreements with her. He had lessened by three-fourths her income to protect himself, and he was now on the highway of departure from the fulfilment of the promises which he had made under circumstances of the most binding character. How did he receive her? He despised her tears, and mocked at her remonstrances. She was in his power, and much did he care whether he would keep his promises or not! Her intervention failed to awaken in his mind any sense of duty. His conscience had become seared as with a red-hot iron. Sir. E. A. kept on in the same heartless course. From day to day, from week to week, he pursued this destructive mode of breaking the back of the business.

Indeed, from this time, persecution of the business became the order of the day. The most shameful opposition to the pursuit of the business was given. Systematic, offensive, and disgraceful means, were used to put an end to the concern. The conspiracy was now organized, and secretly at work, to destroy the business by innumerable petty annoyances and neglects. Threats were made, the most shameful rumours circulated, and all sorts of modes devised to pull down the business. The plot thickened, and the plans of the conspirators culminated; and final efforts were put forth to crush the concern. It was hard to destroy. It had struck its roots deep, and on every side. Its enemies were determined; and at last their purpose was accomplished, and their wicked design was realized.

When the plans of Sir E. A. had ripened, he held a meeting with closed doors, and none were admitted but Mr. W. S., Mr. S. H., and Mr. S. B. It was there and then resolved to put an end to the business. Sir E. A. would not approve a new Manager, stopped the traffic, made no provision to meet the pecuniary engagements of the business, and threatened Mr. J. B. that, if he did not go to the Court of Bankruptcy, they would use compulsory means to force him there. It was the argument of brigands! They attack the peaceful traveller, and, presenting a pistol to his brains, compel him to yield his purse. Although a ward of the Court of Chancery, Mr. J. B. was forced into the Court of Bankruptcy. If all the engagements of the concern had been fulfilled, and all its contracts executed, there would actually have been no trade debts. The money owing was so small, that the concern has often, in its progress, turned over more money in a fortnight, than was due to trade creditors altogether. The creditors were indignant that, for so small a sum, so magnificent a business should be absolutely and utterly sacrificed. The creditors were willing to act in any reasonable manner to prevent this wholesale waste of property. The Trustees, however, persisted in their course. The consequence was, the whole concern was torn up from end to end, the lease surrendered, and the whole plant and material thrown away.

Mr. S. H. had induced Sir E. A. to violate every promise, neglect every engagement, and to set at nought every duty and obligation. Sir E. A., by the advice and at the instigation of this man, descended to the same level of action. Why had all this mischief been done? Why had Mr. S. H. been paid in order to wreak ruin and destruction upon a valuable trade? The envy of Sir E. A. was gratified at the expense of his honesty. He had brought this total ruin upon the son of his friend to shew his power, and that he might exercise his malice; boasting that there was no one to bring him to account, and make him to answer for the wicked deeds of wrong he had done.

Sir E. A. violated the covenants into which he had entered with Mr. J. B. Did he respect the engagement into which he had entered with Mrs. B.? He did not. He had appropriated her property to protect himself from Mr. C. S. S. He had made most solemn promises to her that truth, honour, and uprightness, should govern all his relationships to the business. By cruelty and oppression, he broke away from those most sacred engagements. When he had thus run away from all his engagements, did he return the money he had taken from her? He did not. The Jew had grasped the "pound of flesh," and kept his grasp upon it after he had broken the bond, and never let it go while she lived. Thus Sir E. A. acted towards the widow of Mr. Alderman B.; and, instead of protecting her, did her as much injury as lay in his power; and he never varied in his behaviour till she died. The worst part of his conduct to her consisted in his breach of faith. That he had turned out thus, pressed on her spirits, and eventually broke her heart. If he had acted a just and righteous part, there was every prospect of her living in comfort and honour for many years; but he "brought her grey hairs with sorrow to the grave." It is to the lasting discredit of Mrs. B.'s other friends, that they quietly looked on to see the mischief Sir. E. A. was doing; allowed things to take their course without notice, and did not lift a finger to remonstrate with or prevent him. Thus Sir E. A. had made victims to his ignorance, envy, and malice, of a whole family. He seemed to hate all alike, and all pretty equally. He had made away with a property, equal in all respects to his own. What a disgrace to a man of business to conduct himself in such a manner! He had disobliged an immense number of persons, and could give no account of, and make no excuse for, the unreasonableness of his behaviour. He had managed to bring an insolvency and a bankruptcy upon one of the crack businesses of the city of Manchester. He had no reason to give for his extraordinary behaviour. He was prejudiced against the proprietor; and for this lame cause, he must plot against him, act as a secret and then as an open enemy, and never cease his pursuit until he had thrown down, in a prostrate state before him, the whole concern.

The finale has been to annihilate Mr. J. B's. property, to deprive the legatees under the will of the greater part of theirs, and to victimise the trade creditors. From the treachery of one person has flowed the sacrifice of a great capital, the destruction of a noble business, the dispersion of a large number of industrious persons, causing great individual distress, and the breaking up of valuable business connections.

Mr. S. H. had planned that Sir E. A. should become the possessor of the business. Sir E. A. offered to give one quarter of its value for it. He had deceived the public twice, he had plundered the proprietor and legatees, and the end of it all was, that he might profit by it. For this, he had laboured through such a scene of violence, as had never been known before. Mr. J. B. did not desiderate this fox-and-goose kind of work. He was not anxious to bestow upon Sir E. A. a fortune, for all the abuse, annoyance, mortification, and losses, to which he had been subjected. If Sir E. A. had prospered in his plans, he would have netted £60,000 at once, and made a profit of £10,000 per annum, in permanency. He managed to force the business out of Mr. J. B.'s hands, and to rob him of all the advantage to be derived from it. He could not manage to get legal possession of it for himself. He failed in that. As he could not enjoy it himself, he took care that no one else should be able to do so. He therefore planned its total destruction. This he carried through, and left the place of fruitful industry a complete desert. If he had come at night and set fire to the property, he could not have made a more utter destruction.

No one but those who have experienced it, can tell the difficulty and trouble in establishing, and bringing to perfection, a producing business. Sir E. A. had, however, no consideration for any one or any thing. He must trample upon every one else. The course of Sir E. A. displays the evils of an unrestricted selfishness. He must oppose the current course of events, and the nature of things. He could not be satisfied with things when they were doing well. He must be dissatisfied, and raise difficulties and obstacles, and make himself a nuisance to every body. He could not improve upon what was done. It was not likely. He did not possess the requisite knowledge. How miserable the disposition of the man, who could thus make himself so great a curse!

Nothing can surpass the Court of Bankruptcy for the waste of property. The inferior agents are nothing better than thieves; and the whole system, from beginning to end, is as profligate and unprincipled as can be conceived. The attorney bows to the banker, the valuer to the attorney, and the auctioneer to the public. To part with property through the Bankruptcy Court is looked upon as discreditable, and all becomes a prey for the advantage of those who do not mind the disgrace. Mischief to, and fraud upon, every one, is the order of the day. The plan to cleanse this Augean stable has not yet been devised. It has eluded all the skill and knowledge which have been brought to bear upon it. The state of the law is certainly a disgrace to a civilized community. At this lamentable end did Sir E. A. arrive!

It is very remarkable that Sir E. A. should show to the world how a man ought to behave; and when he had proved his ability to do his duty, he should suddenly turn round, and make himself as awkward and as unpleasant as possible. Through the unlawful violence of Sir E. A., Mr. J. B.'s business was totally destroyed, and his every movement and active efforts were frustrated. No explanation can be offered for the determined and wilful sacrifice of this valuable property. Sir E. A. was resolute in his purpose to make away with the fortune of another man, although nothing but mischief and evil could result from the perpetration of such a crime.

When the concern was placed in the Court of Bankruptcy, Mr. J. B. found insuperable obstacles thrown in the way of any negociation for the resumption of business on honorable grounds. Mr. J. B. was in the peculiar and distressing position of being able to pay every trade debt on the fulfilment of his contracts; and yet, through the inexorable perversity of Sir E. A., his business course was arbitrarily stopped, his contracts broken, his creditors victimized, and himself utterly ruined. Sir E. A. cast into the abyss of bankruptcy the inheritance of another man, the use of which, to its rightful possessor, would have resulted in great pecuniary advantage to himself, and in the performance of all the obligations, by which the proprietor of the business was morally and legally bound.

Mr. J. B. has great reason to be dissatisfied with Mr. W. S. He is a sharp and clever man, and he displayed considerable talent in certain negociations about the business. If he would form his opinions more carefully, defend them more earnestly, and hold them more tenaciously, he would be a first-rate man. From his habits of life, and large practice in cases of insolvency, he is greatly defective in firmness of purpose. He also takes liberties with people he comes in contact with; and no one is safe from his sarcasms. It was a shameful affair, that he should have been a consenting party to the provisions of the management agreement. His want of firmness of purpose was most displayed in abandoning his client in a critical state of his affairs, and going over to the side of his opponents.

In reference to the conduct of Mr. S. H., there is the gravest reason for condemnation. He could not be responsible for Sir E. A.'s peculiar temperament and behaviour. He ought, however, to have acted with honesty, and caution, and regard to the interests of all parties concerned. He manifested the greatest ignorance of trade. His practice is principally that of a conveyancer, and he has a particular aptitude for bullying tenants. Instead of putting forth his energies to make the best of matters, and to improve circumstances for the good of all, by his rashness and recklessness, he has caused the greatest losses of other people's property. To take care of himself is the hourly maxim of his life. Why should he not equally care for his clients? His obstinacy, and impudence, and falsehood, are most outrageous. He shamefully misrepresented the property, and tried publicly to depreciate its value by representing that it was not worth one-tenth of what it had cost. To gain a purpose of his own, he would say anything, and do anything, within the pale of the letter of the law. It is a monstrous state of things, that this man, who need not have £50 as his stock-in trade, should have the opportunity, by his folly and incapacity, to demolish a large mass of property. The talons of such a man ought to be cut, so that he should be prevented from inflicting losses upon persons engaged in commerce. By secretly encouraging the Managers to depart from the direct instructions of the Court of Chancery, by defending those infractions when complained of, and by raising up difficulties in the way of working the concern through neglects and delays, he deserves Mr. J. B.'s most hearty and indignant condemnation. He displayed the worst animus throughout his whole connection with the business. His policy to snatch the concern out of the hands of the proprietor, and throw it into the hands of Sir E. A. was utterly unscrupulous.

It seemed a wrong and irrational piece of conduct for Sir E. A. to go to Mr. S. H. to conduct commercial affairs. It was a wicked thing to go to a man who had no experience and no knowledge of the subject. Mr. S. H. had received no commercial training. He thus precipitated a property, having large capital, into destruction. A business which had gone on prosperously for years, in the hands of this man suddenly collapsed, and immense losses ensued. The work of destruction was his work. Without considering for a moment whether what he was doing was right, he just looked to what was easiest for himself, and according to the letter of the law, and carried on the work of victimising his clients with exultation; boasting of the means he employed, and rejoicing in the misery he was producing, while he saved himself from personal liability.

All Barristers and Attorneys ought to be required to pass a competent examination before being permitted to practise within the domain of commerce. They ought to understand the principles upon which trade depends, and how it ought to be conducted. They ought to be responsible for the right use and application of this knowledge. If any considerable loss of property should accrue by their fault and negligence, an enquiry ought to be instituted, and they should be dealt with accordingly.

The law of forced sale, as at present carried on, is a public scandal. The absolute abomination of persons being compelled to sacrifice an immense fixed property for an inadequate cause, is a system of confiscation and robbery. It is a wicked oppression to compel a man to part with a concern, which has cost a large sum, for a nominal price. There ought to be provided a national Bank by which accommodation might be procured for fixed property, on rates profitable to the Bank, but not absolutely ruinous to parties availing themselves of its accommodation.

It must be acknowledged society has an interest in suppressing all individual oppression. It is said property is worth nothing but what it will fetch in the market. It is no use to offer to sell, if there are no persons able to buy. To be compelled to sell for a tenth or twentieth part of the cost of production is an outrageous injustice. It may be

possible that there may be no persons having sufficient money to pur
chase, or may not choose to purchase, even though it might pay them
to do so. It may answer to work a concern, but not to sell it. Persons ought not to be compelled to sell for a miserably inadequate price
against their own will, or for any sum that Jack, Tom, or Harry, may
happen to fancy to give them.

Mr. S. H. must always be regarded as the active agent in compassing
the great mischief to Mr. J. B. His vanity, violent political opinions,
bitter resentments, and ignorant prejudices, were the causes of his
foolish conduct. He had a fine opportunity to display ability, but he
never could be got to act on the principles of business, but everything
must be transacted according to obsolete and antiquated feudal ideas.

Mr. J. B. finds great fault with the Banker, in refusing trade facilities
for conducting the business, which were important to its welfare. It
was, however, absolutely blameable on the part of Sir E. A. that he
did not overcome the Banker's scruples. If the business was to be
carried on at all, it should have been carried on upon a system essential
to its prosperity. Mr. J. B. also blames the Banker for refusing advan-
ces upon due security being offered. What shall be said of Sir. E. A.'s
not allowing those securities to be negociated elsewhere, but compelling
their sale; thus causing a heavy blow being given to the business,
which he could have averted, without the cost to him of a single shil-
ling? Mr. J. B. also severely blames the Banker for sanctioning Sir E.
A. in the annihilation of a good property; causing a needless loss to
many persons, and destroying the income of a family, whose resources
were invested in the concern, and which were by this means thrown
away, and for no better reason than obstinate spite and peevishness.
The Banker, having acknowledged and sanctioned the procedure of the
business, should have acted harmoniously with that sanction, and acted
unitedly with the Trustees.

There is in the behaviour of a private Banker great danger from
caprice. To-day, you can do business with him; to-morrow, you cannot; then, again, you may do business. The business of a private
Banker is not regulated on any fixed principle, which can be depended
upon. The Bank of England is a kind of public institution, and bears
great sway and influence in money transactions. It is a private cor-
poration under government patronage, influencing the financial
operations of the trade of the country. Banking is a kind of business,
which partakes of a public character. The word of a Banker for a

man, or against a man, goes farther than that of any other trader. As the property of Bankers is all in coin, or bills, or documents, of one kind or another, and as it is always their object to be able to convert these readily, Bankers always sneer at fixed property. They invariably unduly depreciate it. Without fixed property, there could be no floating property. Fixed property becomes useless, when floating property is not in due proportion, to give effect and use to that fixed property.

The modern practice of Bankers, in managing their business, is very different from what it was formerly. All producing businesses are not regarded with favor by Bankers. Their policy is to favor all merchant and agency operations, and to depress the operations of all concerns employing much fixed capital. In times of panic and long depression of trade, there is a danger of fixed properties losing their floating capital, or reducing their capital below the just proportion necessary for the comfortable carrying on of their business. Under such circumstances, the action of Banks upon their present system of management, is enormously to exaggerate the difficulty of conducting business. In the event of a crisis, Banks generally throw their influence on the side of sacrificing a large fixed capital, for the sake of realising a small sum of money.

Checks in business, upon the part of firms having large fixed property, under the united pressure of the Banker and the Attorney, have resulted in losses fabulous in amount; and have reduced the treatment of property, under such circumstances, to a process very much like swindling under the protection of the law. What is the remedy for this state of things? There are two courses to follow. To take out of the hands of government all influence in the monetary arrangements of commerce, and leave them entirely open to public competition. The alternative is, to make Banking a part of the system of government, under the control of a Minister responsible to Parliament. It should be managed like the Post Office, and upon principles regulated upon the statistics of commerce. The system, as at present pursued, is a grinding monopoly, and hangs like a night-mare upon every other trade. To have the business of the country carried on with so small a *bona-fidè* capital, as is now done, involves evils of the greatest magnitude. Whatever the amount of business done, we have only the same amount of floating capital in the country, by which to conduct it. How is the financing, in the ever-varying state of trade, managed? It is done by a system of bills, regulated by the will of the Bankers.

What frightful injuries are suffered and inflicted by this unscrupulous system! Upon the frown or favor of the Bankers, regulated on no imaginable principle, but the passing fancy of the moment, the welfare of thousands of persons, and millions of property depend! The most speculative and rotten concerns have often facilities, while persons possessing ample property are frequently snubbed and inconvenienced for no earthly reason whatever, beyond the whim or the ignorance of the Banker. The most unbearable evils are endured, and with a silence as deep as the grave, simply from the prejudice, or timidity, or hostility, or hatred of the Banker. Let all men be treated impartially, and in such a manner as can be certainly depended on. Business operations may then go on undisturbed by the fear that, after transactions have been effected with all due caution, they may be knocked over in a quarter which has no right to influence them to their prejudice.

Let it be arranged that the proportions of gold and silver employed in banking, be kept in due proportion to the amount of the turnover of the commerce of the country. Business ought not to be convulsed by undue expansions and contractions of the currency. The whole method of public finance ought to be regulated on distinct principles. One fixed amount of the precious metals for a constantly expanding commerce, is evidently absurd. The right amount, for the uses of commerce, ought to be pitched upon according to the returns unfolding the operations of trade, and varied according to the movements of trade. Business ought not to be alternately inflated and depressed by a method more resembling gambling on the one hand, and despotism on the other, than anything like reason and common sense. Money is now professedly under the regulation of the law of the land. Let that law be based on the facts of the case, and be a sound and real exponent of the wants of commerce, and be designed to satisfy those wants.

Mr. W. B. deserves the reprobation of all parties. He was uncle to Mr. J. B., and professed the greatest affection for him. That he should have forgotten all the ties of a close blood-relationship, that he should become unfaithful to his employer to whom he was engaged on a written agreement, that he should be false to the interests of the Legatees whose property he had entered into most solemn engagements to protect, that he should lend himself and make himself a party to the injury of a highly respectable body of creditors, simply that he might be a pander to Sir E. A., is a degradation beyond the power of language to describe. He had been regarded by Mr. J. B. as the familiar friend in whom Mr. J. B. might trust. He acted the part of a Jesuit and a sycophant, that he might curry favour with Sir E. A. He did not even accomplish his object, although he waded knee-deep in servility for its success. Sir E. A. used him as a tool, and then loaded him with contempt. Mr. W. B. disgraced his religious profession, by a course of conduct utterly opposed to the principles of Christianity; and forsook the service of his God, that he might fall down and worship a fallen fellow-creature.

In reference to the exposé of the motives governing the behaviour of Sir E. A., it is a somewhat prolonged task to give a full exhibition. He was the son of poor and godly parents; and had he regarded their instructions, he never would have made shipwreck, in the humiliating manner in which he has done. He was almost entirely uneducated, and possessed that narrowness of mind as the result of poor abilities, and want of proper instruction. In early life he made a religious profession; and during the life of his first wife, never made any striking departures from moral rectitude. He attended the ministry of one of the ablest men who ever occupied a pulpit,—the late Rev. W. Roby, of Manchester. He was surrounded by a number of pious persons, whose example and watchfulness were useful in restraining him from vice. His circumstances continued humble for a prolonged period. Possessing great industry, he toiled unceasingly in the strife for wealth. Gradually the passion for gold became exorbitant. It was said of him, that he pushed aside everything for its sake. His family, his religion, and his mental improvement, all suffered. Money he would have 'at any price; and he got it; and sacrificed for that, his intellectual, moral, and spiritual interests. Hence, for thirty years, his pecuniary interests have been advancing, while his general character has been retrograding. Instead of a general development of the whole man, there has been growth in the acquisition of money, and declining vigour in the most weighty matters.. As a man, a friend, and a Christian, there has been faithful and progressive deterioration; and, like Demas, for the sake of the things of this world, he has forsaken the kingdom of Christ. He became less particular in the regulation of his conduct. He began to oppress and grind the poor; and for many years his place of business was in the most degraded moral condition. He has thus degenerated from the profession of Christianity into the apostate, the hypocrite, and the worldling.

This unhappy man, in conjunction with Mr. W. B., became, in an evil hour, the Trustee for the estate of the late Mr. Alderman B. The world has never beheld two men who have more egregiously failed in the discharge of their duty. From the very first, Sir E. A. manifested a litigious disposition, and shewed symptoms of levity and carelessness, proving his friendship to be of a very precarious nature, and based on very slippery foundations. In his relationships with the concern, he shewed no tact or prudence. His only idea seemed to be to save himself from trouble and responsibility. His manner of acting had the most prejudicial effect. He shewed to every one, with whom he came in contact, that nothing could be expected from his friendship. He exercised an injurious influence on the minds of all persons who had relationships with the business, and shewed a want of determination to back the concern. This mean and contemptible spirit was displayed through the greater part of his career. He had the power to benefit the business, but the captiousness of his temper caused him to recoil from the discharge of his duty. Whatever could induce a man with his feelings to become a Trustee, is an enigma. Whether he was in ignorance of the nature of the duties he would have to discharge, or whether the difference of the business to that to which he was accustomed galled him, cannot be stated; but, from some cause or other, the irritability of his temper was aroused, and in general kept at a boiling temperature. Sir E. A. was a source of constant anxiety; and there was continual need for watchfulness, lest he should break out into some wild extravagance or other, and commit injuries which never could be repaired. Notwithstanding every care, at the time of the Russian war, he broke through every restraint; and without a single effort to evade a difficulty, without a day's notice of what he intended to do, he stopped the traffic, and forced on to the concern a process of insolvency; and through his perverseness, brought down a deluge of evils, from which there has not been a moment's intermission from that day to this.

He was appointed a Trustee for the protection of the property. It was supposed, from his character as a man of business, there would have been some security for the due and intelligent administration of affairs. No greater hallucination could exist. He allowed himself to become a mere puppet in the hands of Mr. S. H.; and all the more dangerous, because he acted the puppet. He was called to act in a sphere for which he was alike unfitted to act by education, habit, and opinion, and he thereby produced the greatest disasters. He professed to know his own business, and yet in another man's business he outraged every principle of common sense. On-lookers were shocked at his conduct. His excuses to his victims, and to persons friendly to them, when they saw what they could scarcely believe although they saw it, and intreated him to interfere and prevent further mischief, were, " I am not responsible," and, " I act under legal advice." He expected such an answer would silence all objections, and quench all remonstrances. As he was in a good position, he found encouragement in certain quarters; and they would reply to his statements, and say in a chorus, " You·could not have acted otherwise, Sir E." He thus became an active agent to destroy that property which it was his office to protect.

When Sir E. A. became possessed of unrestrained power over the concern, and everything was done at his bidding, there was not the slightest improvement in his treatment of the business. Despots generally improve their administration, when they have knocked over all their rivals. The reckless conduct of Sir E. A. was never more plainly exhibited, than in the management of the business, after he had obtained supreme power in its direction. Fear often produces cruelty. The dread of losing his own property was so great as to reduce him to a most pitiable condition, and rendered him utterly unfeeling towards the interests of other persons. His sensitiveness, lest he should compromise himself in the opinion of the world, delayed him for a time in his wicked path.

His conduct since the catastrophe has been marked by the prevailing characteristics which regulated his behaviour antecedent to that event. It has consisted in an endeavour to justify himself by a perversion of the facts of the case, and an attempt to throw upon others the blame of what he had done himself. In doing this, he has been altogether unscrupulous. Indeed, his violation of the truth was so flagrant, as to be plain to every one who had any opportunity to compare one part of his conduct with another. He had used his tongue as a shield for himself. He desired to place everything in a false light before others, and to resist any claims which might be made upon him from the sufferers by his conduct. The intervention of old acquaintances and friends to excite in his mind a sense of repentance for the evils he has done, have been useless and inefficacious. His heart is too hard, his head is too stolid, his temper too false and treacherous, and his character too degraded, for such means to have anything more than a nominal effect. He would give sweet words, make the most gracious promises, and break them without the slightest regard even to appearances. A prolonged period has been given him for reflection; all his fallacies have been exposed and condemned, and he has been driven into a corner; and his only refuge has been in the most wilful misstatement, the most reckless indifference, and the haughtiest defiance.

What is the just treatment of such men, and what should be their punishment? Shall they be allowed to plan the greatest crimes, and carry them out, and then be excused from all punishment? Is it for the interest of society that such a course should be adopted? Is it not right that men who violate the laws of their country should be made to answer for what they have done, and stand the consequences of their offences? Is a man, because he is rich, to be permitted to rob others, and no mention to be made of his theft? Shall Sir E. A. be called upon to compensate those whom he has wantonly injured, and whose rights and properties he has trampled upon and annihilated? He has outraged the laws of his country. It is for the judicature of the country to pronounce upon his behaviour, and to say what shall be done to him.

THE END.